W9-AAL-688

HEiDi HECKELBECK
Is Not a Thief!

By Wanda Coven
Illustrated by Priscilla Burris

LITTLE SIMON
New York London Toronto Sydney New Delhi

LITTLE SIMON
An imprint of Simon & Schuster Children's Publishing Division
1230 Avenue of the Americas, New York, New York 10020
First Little Simon hardcover edition January 2015
Copyright © 2015 by Simon & Schuster, Inc.
Also available in a Little Simon paperback edition.
All rights reserved, including the right of reproduction in whole or in part in any form.
LITTLE SIMON is a registered trademark of Simon & Schuster, Inc., and associated colophon is a trademark of Simon & Schuster, Inc.
For information about special discounts for bulk purchases, please contact Simon & Schuster Special Sales at 1-866-506-1949 or business@simonandschuster.com.
The Simon & Schuster Speakers Bureau can bring authors to your live event. For more information or to book an event contact the Simon & Schuster Speakers Bureau at 1-866-248-3049 or visit our website at www.simonspeakers.com.
Designed by Ciara Gay
Manufactured in the United States of America 1214 FFG
10 9 8 7 6 5 4 3 2 1
Library of Congress Cataloging-in-Publication Data
Coven, Wanda.
Heidi Heckelbeck is not a thief! / by Wanda Coven ; illustrated by Priscilla Burris. — First edition.
pages cm. — (Heidi Heckelbeck ; #13)
Summary: Accused of stealing her best friend's cool new pen, young witch Heidi Heckelbeck must turn to her *Book of Spells* to clear her name.
ISBN 978-1-4814-2324-3 (pbk) — ISBN 978-1-4814-2325-0 (hc) —
ISBN 978-1-4814-2326-7 (eBook) [1. Friendship—Fiction. 2. Pens—Fiction. 3. Witches—Fiction. 4. Magic—Fiction.] I. Burris, Priscilla, illustrator. II. Title.
PZ7.C83393Him 2015
[Fic]—dc23
2014003871

CONTENTS

Yum!

Yummy!

Yumsicles!

Heidi Heckelbeck loved pizza day. She slid a hot slice of pepperoni pizza onto her lunch tray. Then she sat down with her friends Lucy

Lancaster and Bruce Bickerson.

"I have great news!" said Bruce.

"What?" asked Heidi and Lucy at the same time.

Bruce looked around to make sure no one was listening. Then he lowered his voice to a whisper. "My latest invention is finished!" he said. "But don't tell anyone. It's top secret!"

Bruce's inventions were always top secret. He didn't want anyone to steal his ideas, but he trusted his two best friends, Heidi and Lucy.

"What's it called?" asked Heidi excitedly.

Bruce leaned forward so only the girls could hear. The girls leaned in too.

"I'm calling it the Bicker Picker-Upper," he whispered.

"What does it do?" Lucy asked.

"It picks stuff up *automatically*," said Bruce.

"Like a robot?" asked Heidi.

"Like a robot's arm," Bruce said.

"What kinds of things does it pick up?" asked Lucy.

"Stuffed animals, action figures, socks, underwear, pajamas—basically everything on my floor," said Bruce.

"It picks up your room?" Heidi

questioned as she took a big bite of pizza. "THIS I gotta see!"

"Me too!" said Lucy.

"Can you guys come over after school tomorrow?" asked Bruce.

"Probably," said Heidi.

"I'll check with my mom," Lucy said. Then she pulled her baby owl notepad from her backpack.

Lucy also took out a pink pen shaped like a lollipop. The lollipop had a spiral design and sparkled with pink and silver glitter.

She wrote a reminder
on her notepad:

Ask permission to
go to Bruce's house
tomorrow

The lollipop lit up as she wrote.
Heidi dropped her pizza on her lunch
tray and stared at Lucy's pen.

"WHERE did you get THAT?" asked
Heidi.

Lucy twirled the pen in front of her
friends.

"Isn't it beautiful?" she said. "My dad brought it back from his last business trip."

"I LOVE it!" said Heidi. "May I see?"
"Sure!" Lucy said.

But just then the bell rang. It was time to go back to the classroom. Lucy dropped the pen into her backpack.

"I'd better show you at recess," she said.

"But I want to see it NOW!" Heidi complained.

Lucy laughed. "I promise I'll show you LATER!"

"Oh, okay," said Heidi.

Then they cleared their trays and
headed down the hall.

Chapter 2

YUMDiNGERS!

At recess Heidi, Bruce, and Lucy sat on the steps at the edge of the playground. Lucy pulled out her lollipop pen and notepad.

"Watch this," she said.

Lucy drew a smiley face. Again, as soon as she pressed the tip of the pen against the notepad, the topper began to glow and the glitter sparkled even more.

"That is SO cool!" Heidi said. She couldn't take her eyes off the lollipop pen.

"It even has a strawberry scent," said Lucy, holding the pen under Heidi's nose.

Heidi took a big whiff. *"Mmm,"* she said dreamily.

Then Bruce took a sniff. "Smells fruity!" he said.

"May I PLEASE try it now?" begged Heidi.

Lucy handed the pen to Heidi.  Heidi drew a turtle on Lucy's notepad. Then she drew a daisy.

"Okay, that does it!" declared Heidi. "I HAVE to have one!"

"Now let ME have a turn!" said Bruce.

Heidi handed the pen to Bruce. He took off his glasses and studied the pen. Then he tested it.

"The technology is quite simple," he said. "I'll bet I can make one of these in my lab."

"MAKE one?" questioned Lucy.

"Sure," said Bruce. He handed the pen back to Lucy.

"I'll settle for a store-bought one," said Heidi. "I can't wait that long."

Lucy suddenly gave Heidi and Bruce a little nudge.

They looked up and saw Melanie Maplethorpe and Stanley Stone-wrecker walking toward them.

Melanie thought she, herself, was so great. It drove Heidi crazy.

"What's going on over here?" asked Melanie. "Not that I really care or anything."

"Lucy has got a cool new pen," said Heidi.

Melanie looked at the pen in Lucy's hand. "What's so great about a lollipop pen?" she asked snootily.

"Watch this," said Lucy. Then she began to write on her notepad.

O My pen glows when
I write with it!

Melanie's eyes grew wide when she saw the glittery pen sparkle and glow when Lucy used it. She loved *anything* that sparkled.

"See?" said Heidi. "Isn't that the coolest pen EVER?"

Melanie ignored Heidi. She would never admit that she liked anything Heidi liked. But Stanley didn't mind saying so.

"Yumdingers!" he exclaimed. "That pen looks good enough to EAT!"

Chapter 3

I OWE YOU!

Mom and Aunt Trudy already had dinner going when Heidi got home from school. Aunt Trudy often had dinner with the Heckelbecks.

"You'll never guess what!" shouted Heidi as she walked through the door.

Mom held two dry lasagna noodles

up to her ears. "Indoor voice!" she said.

"Sorry," said Heidi.

"Okay, what's your big news?" Mom asked as she layered a ribbon of lasagna noodle over some meat sauce.

"Lucy got a new pen!" said Heidi breathlessly. "It's a lollipop that lights

up and sparkles and everything! May I get one?"

Mom frowned.

"PLEASE?" begged Heidi. "I want one more than anything in the whole world!"

Aunt Trudy chuckled as she sliced cucumbers for the salad. "Lucy's pen sounds pretty neat!" she said.

"It IS!" said Heidi, washing her hands at the sink. "The topper even smells like strawberries!"

Heidi tossed a handful of toasted almonds and cranberries into the salad.

"I'm sure it's an *incredible* pen," said Mom. "But you can't always expect to get the latest new thing."

"That's true," agreed Aunt Trudy. "But I do need to pay Heidi and Henry for helping me repot my herb plants. This might be the perfect thing."

"Did you hear that?" sang Heidi as she did a little victory dance.

"It's payday!" Then she thought for a moment. "But Henry won't want a sparkly light-up lollipop pen that smells like strawberries."

Henry walked into the room. "What wouldn't I want?" he asked.

"A sparkly lollipop pen that lights up," said Heidi.

"*Ding! Ding!* That answer is CORRECT!" said Henry, sounding like a game show host. "Do I win a prize?"

"Yup! You just won yourself a SUCKER pen!" said Heidi.

"Very funny," said Henry.

"Okay, if you could have any kind of pen you wanted—what would you pick?" asked Heidi.

Henry tapped the side of his head with his pointer finger. "I know!" he said. "I'd pick a pirate sword pen!"

"Then it's settled," said Aunt Trudy. "I'll look for a lollipop pen and a pirate sword pen at Lena's Crafts tomorrow."

"Well, blimey, sis!" cried Henry. "Methinks we struck it rich!"

Chapter 4

TWiNS

Heidi grabbed Lucy by the arm as they entered the classroom the next morning. "My mom said I could get a lollipop pen just like yours!" she said excitedly.

"Then we'll be TWINS!" Lucy said.

"It'll be so fun!" said Heidi.

The girls squealed and jumped up and down.

During language arts, Lucy wrote a poem about her new lollipop pen. Mrs. Welli, their teacher, asked her to recite it in front of the class. Lucy stood up and showed her pen so

everyone could see it. Then she read
her poem.

My new pen has the
shape of a lollipop.
It looks like something
from a candy shop!
It smells like fruit, and
it matches my clothes.
And when I write, the
lollipop glows!

Everyone clapped.
"Well done!" said
Mrs. Welli. "What a
clever poem!"

Heidi wanted to write a poem when she got her lollipop pen too. On the bus ride home from school she began to think about how it would go.

The bus lurched to a stop. Heidi jumped out and ran all the way home. Henry was waiting for her at the door.

"Finally!" Henry said.

"Is she here yet?" asked Heidi.

"Just got here!" said Henry.

They charged into the kitchen.

"Hi, Aunt Trudy!" said Heidi the moment she saw her aunt. "Do you have the pens?"

"Hi, kids!" said Aunt Trudy. "Let me see. I just may have something for you two. . . ."

She pulled a small paper bag out from behind her back.

Heidi and Henry shrieked and

raced toward Aunt Trudy. Mom sighed and set grilled cheese sandwich strips and tomato soup on the table.

"Close your eyes and hold out your hands," said Aunt Trudy.

The children did as their aunt asked.

"No peeking!" Aunt Trudy said.

Heidi heard the paper bag crinkle. Then she felt the shape of a lollipop pen in her hand.

"Open your eyes!"

Heidi and Henry opened their eyes.

"Shiver me timbers!" said Henry when he saw his pirate sword pen. "I love it!" He pretended to have a swordfight. Then he poked

Heidi in the back with the tip of the pen.

"Stop it!" complained Heidi.

Henry jumped back.

"What's YOUR problem?" he asked.

Heidi plunked down on a chair and put the purple lollipop pen on the table. It had swirls just like Lucy's, but it didn't have any glitter,

it didn't light up, and it didn't even have a fruity scent.

"Oh dear," said Aunt Trudy. "Did I get the wrong one?"

Heidi didn't want to hurt her aunt's feelings. "No," she said quietly. "It was really nice of you to get me a lollipop pen."

But Aunt Trudy could tell Heidi was disappointed.

"I'll keep looking," her aunt said.

But Heidi doubted her aunt would find a pen like Lucy's. After all, Lucy's father bought it somewhere far away.

Heidi swirled a grilled cheese stick in her tomato soup. *Now Lucy and I won't get to be twins after all,* she thought.

Chapter 5

GENiUS AT WORK

Honk! Honk!

"It's the Lancasters," said Heidi's mother.

Heidi and Lucy were supposed to go to Bruce's house that afternoon. Now Heidi didn't feel much like going. She dragged herself out the door.

When they got to the Bickersons',
Bruce and his dog, Frankie, greeted
the girls at the door. Bruce had on
his white lab coat and safety glasses.

Frankie wagged his tail and ran in circles around the girls. Lucy knelt down and scratched Frankie behind the ears. Heidi watched glumly.

"What's the matter, Heidi?" asked Lucy as she stood up. "You've been quiet ever since we picked you up."

Heidi sighed. "Sorry," she said. "It's just that my aunt bought me a lollipop pen and it doesn't light up, sparkle, or smell good, like yours."

"That's too bad," said Lucy.

"Can I see yours again?" asked Heidi.

"Sure," said Lucy. She pulled the pen from her backpack. Heidi studied it longingly.

"I can still MAKE you one," offered Bruce.

Heidi handed the pen back to Lucy. "That's okay," she said.

"Speaking of inventions," said Lucy as she carefully put her pen back in her backpack, "let's see Bruce's famous Bicker Picker-Upper!"

"I thought you'd never ask!" he said excitedly.

Bruce led the girls to the basement door. The air smelled damp and musty as they thumped down the wooden stairs. He guided them into his laboratory.

"Welcome to the Den of Discovery!" he said proudly. "Also known as the Bickerson Lab."

Bruce had a workbench with a microscope, beakers, flasks full of liquids, a test tube rack, and a gooseneck lamp. A poster on the workbench wall read GENIUS AT WORK. Bruce dragged over stools for Heidi and Lucy to sit on. Then he picked

up a black metal box with a joystick on top.

"Now this simple device is the soon-to-be world-famous Bicker Picker-Upper," said Bruce in a very scientific-sounding voice.

Heidi and Lucy clapped.

"I shall demonstrate how to use this simple device," Bruce went on. "Notice the blue plastic ball on the floor."

The girls nodded. Then Bruce sat on a stool.

"I will retrieve the ball without leaving this stool. Watch closely."

Bruce pushed the joystick forward. The box whizzed and whirred, and a long metal arm began to stretch forward. When the arm reached the

ball, Bruce pushed a button. A metal claw at the end of the arm opened up. He touched the button again and the claw grabbed hold of the ball. Then Bruce pulled back on the joystick and the arm retracted back toward the box. He released the ball into his hand and held it up.

"Voilà!" he said.

"Hey, it actually works!" said Heidi.

"Of course it works!" Bruce said.

"It reminds me of the claw arcade game," said Lucy.

"Similar technology," said Bruce. "You want to try?"

The girls took turns picking up
the ball. Then they tried to pick up
other things, like
Frankie's dog
toys, a fuzzy
slipper, and

a large action figure.

"Bruce, someday you're going to be famous," said Heidi.

"I want to invent something that changes the world," said Bruce.

"Like what?" asked Lucy.

"I'm not sure yet," said Bruce. "But I want to do something BIG."

"You will," said Lucy.

"Until then, let's play Ping-Pong," suggested Heidi.

Bruce and Lucy laughed. They played Ping-Pong until Heidi's dad came to pick them up.

Chapter 6

ARE YOU MAD?

Heidi ran across the playground toward Lucy and Bruce. She shielded her eyes from the morning sun.

"Hey, guys!" she said cheerfully.

"Hey," said Bruce.

"I had a blast at your house yesterday," Heidi said.

"Me too," said Bruce.

Heidi looked at Lucy. "Wasn't it fun?" she asked.

Lucy looked the other way.

"What's the matter, Lucy?" asked Heidi.

"Nothing," her friend said coldly.

Heidi looked at Bruce to see if he knew anything. Bruce looked at the ground.

Heidi turned back to Lucy. "What's going on?" she pressed.

Lucy lowered her eyebrows and pushed her lips together. "As if you didn't know," she said.

"What are you talking about?" asked Heidi.

"Okay, I'll tell you," Lucy said crossly. "My lollipop pen is missing!

It wasn't in my backpack when I got home last night."

Heidi blinked in disbelief.

"So please give it BACK, right now!" Lucy said firmly.

"But I don't have it," said Heidi. "Maybe it fell out of your backpack at Bruce's."

"I checked all over," Bruce said, "but I couldn't find it."

"Maybe it's in my dad's car," suggested Heidi.

"Nice try," Lucy said.

"What's THAT supposed to mean?" asked Heidi.

"Think about it," said Lucy. "You wanted a lollipop pen, then your aunt didn't get you the right one—and now mine is MISSING!"

Heidi's face fell. "You really think I stole your pen?" she asked.

Lucy looked away for a moment. "Well, it sure looks that way," she said.

"Wow," said Heidi. "What kind of friend do you think I am?"

Lucy just turned and walked away.

Chapter 7

RAZZLE-DAZZLE!

Heidi and Lucy didn't speak to each other the rest of the day. At recess Lucy walked off with Natalie Newman. In science Lucy picked Bruce to be her partner. Heidi couldn't wait for the day to end.

Heidi dropped her backpack on the

floor when she got home. The loud *ker-thunk* got Mom's attention. She looked at Heidi's long face.

"What's the matter, pumpkin?" she asked gently.

Heidi sighed heavily and plunked

onto a kitchen chair. "Lucy thinks I took her lollipop pen," she said. "But I didn't."

Mom sat down beside Heidi. "Can I help you find it?" she asked.

"Maybe," said Heidi. "She lost it

somewhere between Bruce's house and her house. Can we check Dad's car?"

"Sure," said Mom. "Dad's working at home in his lab today, so his car is in the garage."

Heidi's face brightened. "Can we check right now?"

Mom nodded. She grabbed Dad's keys, and they headed for the garage.

They searched between the seats and
under the seats—they even looked
under the floor mats. But all they
found were two Goldfish crackers, a
take-out napkin, and a quarter.

Heidi walked slowly back into the house and flopped onto the couch in the family room. *Maybe I should*

ask Bruce to make Lucy a new pen, she thought. *Then Lucy and I can be friends again.* That gave Heidi an even better idea. *What if I make a new pen for Lucy?*

Heidi jumped from the couch and zoomed to her backpack. She pulled out the lollipop pen Aunt Trudy had given to her and examined it closely. *There must be a spell that can make this pen as cool as Lucy's.*

Heidi ran upstairs

and pulled out her *Book of Spells* and her Witches of Westwick medallion from under her bed. She studied the Contents page and found a chapter called Jazz It Up! Under that she found a spell called Fancy Utensils! She flipped the pages and read the spell.

Fancy Utensils!

Are your forks and knives plain and boring? Do your serving spoons need pizzazz? Could your writing utensils use some razzle-dazzle? Then this is the spell for you!

Ingredients:

2 dashes of glitter

2 cups of fruit punch

1 ice cube

Mix the ingredients together in a shallow baking pan. Completely cover the utensil with the mix. Hold your Witches of Westwick medallion in one hand and place the other over the pan. Chant the following spell:

SHiMMy, WHiMMy, ZiP, ZaP, ZiNG!
GiVE THiS [NaME OF UTENSiL] LiGHTS aND BLiNG!

Note: If you want your utensil to have a fruity scent, add this chant to your spell:

Shazoo! Shazee! Shazell!
Give this [Name of utensil]
a fruity smell!

Heidi bookmarked the page. *This should do the trick!* she thought.

Chapter 8

A NEW TWIST

Heidi crept down the stairs. She leaned over the banister and listened. She heard her mother on the phone in her office. She already knew Henry was in his room and Dad was in his lab.

Then Heidi tiptoed quickly into

the kitchen and got to work. She grabbed a shallow brownie pan and a measuring cup. Then she scanned the shelves in the pantry for fruit punch. *Nothing in here,* she thought.

Heidi looked in the fridge, but all they had was lemonade and orange juice. *I know,* she thought. *I'll mix them together and make my own fruit punch!* She poured a cup of lemonade into the pan, followed by a cup of

orange juice. Then she plopped an ice cube into the mix.

Heidi covered the pan with a plastic lid, grabbed a big spoon, and hurried to the craft closet in the downstairs hallway. She rummaged through bins of pipe cleaners, pom-poms, and rubber stamps.

Then she dug out
some red glitter.
Good enough, she
thought. She shoved
the tube of red glitter
into her skirt pocket
and carried the pan to
her room. Heidi shut the
door with the back of her sneaker.

She set the pan on the floor and
pulled off the lid. She carefully
squeezed two dashes of glitter into

the mix. Heidi stirred the ingredients with the spoon. Then she laid her lollipop pen in the pan so that it was covered with the magical potion.

Next Heidi slipped her Witches of Westwick medallion over her head. She grasped the medallion in one hand and held the other over the mix. Then she chanted the spell and added the scent part of the spell. The mix bubbled beneath the palm of her hand and settled. Heidi peeked into the pan.

"Oh my gosh!" she cried as she pulled the pen out of the pan. "What happened?"

The lollipop pen had twisted into the shape of a pretzel and blinked like some kind of crazy Christmas light. Heidi sniffed it. It smelled lemony

and orangey. *Well, it sparkles and it smells good,* thought Heidi. *But now you can't write with it.*

"Merg," she growled. "I should've used real fruit punch."

Chapter 9

IN THE DOGHOUSE

Heidi heard a soft knock on her door. "Who is it?"

"It's Mom," said her mother as she opened the door. She walked into the room with an armful of laundry. Her eyes went right to the pan and the *Book of Spells* on the floor.

"What on earth are you up to?" asked Mom—even though she knew *exactly* what was going on.

Heidi turned around. "I know I'm not supposed to use my witching skills without asking," Heidi said gloomily. "But I wanted to make a new lollipop

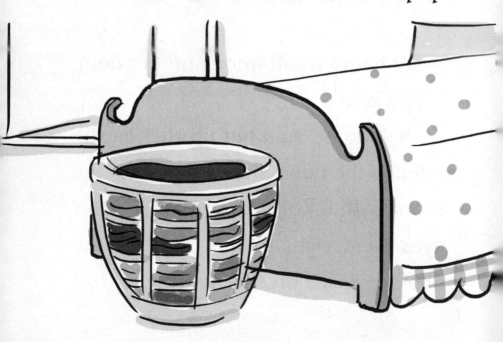

pen for Lucy so we could be friends again. And look what happened."

She held out the sparkly, blinking pretzel pen for her mother to see. Mom didn't scold Heidi. She put down the laundry and sat down beside her daughter.

"It doesn't matter," Mom said. "Pen or no pen, you and Lucy will be friends again."

"It sure doesn't seem like it," said Heidi.

"Give her some time," suggested Mom. "She needs to think things over."

"But she thinks I'm a THIEF!" said Heidi. "And that really hurts my feelings."

"The truth will come out," said Mom.

Then the phone began to ring. Mom got up and dashed down the hall to answer it. She came back with the phone. She covered the receiver with her hand.

"It's Bruce," whispered Mom. "He wants to know if you'd like to come over and play Frisbee."

"May I?" asked Heidi.

"Sure," Mom said. "I think a little fresh air and a playdate are just what you need."

She handed the phone to Heidi.

"Hi, Bruce," Heidi said. "I'll be right over."

Mom dropped off Heidi at the Bickersons'. Bruce and Frankie

were waiting out front.

"Let's play in the backyard," said
Bruce.

Heidi followed Bruce through the
side gate. Then they tossed the Frisbee
back and forth. Frankie barked and
tried to get the Frisbee.

"Is Lucy still mad at you?" asked Bruce, throwing the Frisbee backhand.

"Pretty much," said Heidi as she caught the disk. "She still thinks I stole her lollipop pen." She tossed the Frisbee back to Bruce.

"That stinks," said Bruce as he hurled the Frisbee toward Heidi.

The Frisbee soared over Heidi's head and out of reach. Frankie raced after it and grabbed the disk between his teeth. Then he scampered across the yard to his doghouse.

"Hey, come back here!" cried Bruce as he chased after his dog.

Bruce got down on his knees. Then he crawled halfway into the doghouse.

"Heidi!" Bruce shouted. "Come here!"

Heidi ran over and knelt beside the doghouse. Bruce handed Heidi the Frisbee and slowly backed out. Then he got to his feet.

"I have caught the thief!" Bruce exclaimed.

He had Lucy's lollipop pen in his hand.

Chapter 10

CLiCK!

Heidi squealed and grabbed the pen.

"Bruce, you're a LIFESAVER!" cried Heidi as she jumped up and down.

"Just a day in the life of a super-hero," said Bruce.

Heidi laughed. "Let's call Lucy," she said.

They ran in through the back door.
Bruce grabbed the phone and handed
it to Heidi. She dialed Lucy's number,

which she knew by heart.
The phone rang for *forever*.

Mrs. Lancaster finally
answered.

"Hello. Is Lucy there?"
asked Heidi.

Mrs. Lancaster put Lucy
on the line.

"Hello?" said Lucy.

"We found your pen!" Heidi blurted out.

Then Lucy screamed. Heidi held the receiver out so Bruce could hear.

"I think she's happy," said Heidi.

"Just a little," said Bruce, laughing.

"WHERE?" asked Lucy.

"Bruce found it in Frankie's DOGHOUSE!" said Heidi. "It has a couple of teeth marks, but it still works perfectly."

"I'll be right over!" Lucy said, hanging up the phone.

✦ ⋆ ✳ ◎ ⋆

Bruce and Heidi ran across the lawn to greet Lucy.

Heidi pulled the lollipop pen from her back pocket. "Here," she said.

Lucy looked at the pen in disbelief, but she didn't take it. "I want you to have it," she said.

Heidi looked at the pen longingly. "No," she said, handing the pen to Lucy. "This is YOUR special pen, and

I don't ever want it to come between us again."

"I'm so sorry, Heidi," said Lucy. "I should've known you weren't a thief. I feel terrible."

"That's okay," Heidi said. "I'm just

glad we can be friends again."

The girls hugged.

Then Heidi's mother pulled up in the driveway with Aunt Trudy. The

girls ran to the car window. Bruce and Frankie followed behind.

"Bruce found Lucy's pen!" said Heidi.

"Thank goodness!" Mom said.

"I found something too," said Aunt Trudy.

She handed a small brown paper
bag to Heidi. Heidi peeked in the bag
and pulled out a green lollipop pen, a

purple lollipop pen, and a lightsaber
pen. All of them lit up—just like

Lucy's. Heidi sniffed the lollipop pens.
Green apple and grape.

She squealed.

"Where did you
find them?" she
asked.

"Not telling,"
Aunt Trudy said
with a witchy wink.

Heidi handed the grape lollipop pen to Lucy and the lightsaber pen to Bruce. Then she raised her green lollipop pen in the air.

"To best friends!" she said.

Lucy and Bruce held up their pens.

"To best friends!" they cheered.

"Okay, everyone strike a pose!" said Mom as she held up her camera phone.

The friends held out their new pens and made goofy faces.

"Now say 'Heidi Heckelbeck is *not* a thief!'" Mom said.

"HEIDI HECKELBECK IS *NOT* A THIEF!" they shouted. Then they busted up laughing.

Click!

And Mom got a very *sweet* photo.

Check out the next book starring

Wiggle!

Jiggle!

Jaggle!

Heidi stood on a kitchen chair and looked in the mirror that hung by the back door. Mom used this mirror to put on lipstick before she left the house. Heidi used it to look at her loose tooth.

An excerpt from *Heidi Heckelbeck Says "Cheese!"*

"Oh no!" she exclaimed. "It's SUPER-loose!"

"Which one is it?" asked Mom.

Heidi turned around on the chair and put her finger on her tooth. "My fwunt one!" she said.

She wiggled it again.

"Wow, that *is* really loose," agreed Mom.

"Well, it had better not fall out!" Heidi declared.

Mom looked puzzled. "Why not?"

"Because Picture Day at school is in TWO days," Heidi said. "And I don't want a big hole in my smile."

An excerpt from *Heidi Heckelbeck Says "Cheese!"*

"Then stop wiggling it," suggested Mom.

"That's easy for you to say!" Heidi said, poking her tooth with her tongue.

"Get your mind on something else," said Mom.

Heidi tried to think about something else. She looked at the ceiling and rubbed her chin thoughtfully. Then she sighed.

"It's no use," she said. "All I can think about is my loose tooth."

An excerpt from *Heidi Heckelbeck Says "Cheese!"*